Magical Mayhem

Part Four

To Prevent Smart Choices

Emily Martha Sorensen

Also by Emily Martha Sorensen

Standalones:
Black Magic Academy

The End in the Beginning:
The Keeper and the Rulership
The Fires of the Rulership
The Magic or the Rulership

Fairy Senses:
Fairy Eyeglasses
Fairy Compass
Fairy Earmuffs
Fairy Barometer
Fairy Pox
Fairy Slippers
Fairy Lunchbox
Fairy Icepack

Trilogy of a Teenage Werevulture:
Trials of a Teenage Werevulture

The Numbers Just Keep
Getting Bigger:
Twenty-Four Potential
Children of Prophecy

Dragon Eggs:
Dragon's Egg
Dragon's Hope
Dragon's First Christmas
Dragon's Fire

Magical Mayhem:
To Prevent World Peace
To Prevent Chic Costumes
To Prevent Clear Paths

Comics:
A Magical Roommate
To Prevent World Peace

Short Story Collections:
Worlds of Wonder

Picture Books:
Tabby, Tabby, Burning Bright

To Prevent Smart Choices

To Frederik Vendelin,

longtime fan of the comic,
reader of my other books,
and Patreon supporter.

Chapter 1
The Eavesdrop

Paint dribbled from the thick brush as Kendra swiped it from one side of the crack to the other. *Swipe swipe swipe.*

"...So I don't think Florence is going to come," Kendra concluded, finishing the interminable story that had felt like it was never going to wrap up.

"Good," Chronos grunted from below her.

"*Good?*" Kendra's head spun around, glaring down at her. "Florence said no, and you say *good?*"

Chronos dunked her thick brush into the can of housepaint beside her. Truth be told, she hadn't listened for the last ten minutes, but she wasn't going to admit that. If she did, Kendra might feel the need to explain the whole spiel all over again from the beginning.

"You were asking her to join you, right?" Chronos hazarded. The last thing she had paid attention to was Kendra going over a long list of reasons why Florence would have made a perfect member of their still-unnamed villain team.

"Yes!" Kendra said impatiently. "Weren't you listening?"

No, Chronos thought.

"Yes," she said.

"Well," Kendra said huffily, shoving her paintbrush into the can of paint perched precariously on top of the ladder she was standing upon, "then you should know there's nothing good about it. We *needed* Florence!"

"Then maybe you should've told her that before you quit your team and left her behind," Chronos said tartly, jabbing her paintbrush into the cracks in the paint beside her.

She was feeling rather cranky to be doing this chore in the first place. Tiffany's "FIX IT!" power had fixed the structural damage on the outside walls of the lair, but the paint had stayed cracked, leaving exposed stone and bricks underneath. Chronos hadn't even noticed that, much less cared, but Kendra had shown up in her bedroom this morning with two paintbrushes and cans of paint.

"C'mon, oracle!" Kendra had said impatiently. *"We have to make this place look respectable!"*

"Why?" Chronos had asked incredulously. *"Who's going to see it?"*

Logic hadn't worked on Kendra, however, and then next thing she'd known, they were both outside painting walls for no good reason whatsoever.

That girl is way too obsessed with appearances, Chronos thought grumpily, poking her paintbrush into the holes in the paint and moving down a step to reach the next part. *I hope she and Rhea never meet.*

"...which was why I couldn't tell her then," Kendra was saying. "But of course I thought of it! I knew we would need Florence! She has powers to incapacitate without injuring, and she wouldn't have had to give them up because she was in no danger of turning evil! What do you take me for?"

A person who can't stop talking long enough to notice that I'm not listening? Chronos thought.

"Oh, I know what you're thinking," Kendra said, glaring as she swiped her paintbrush back and forth again across the spot that was already perfectly smooth. "'That's just an excuse! She just wanted her best friend back on a team with her!' But that's not it! We needed her!"

Is she ever going to stop talking? Chronos wondered.

"Because we need her powers," Kendra went on. "Nobody else on the team has magic!"

Chronos stopped painting to stare upwards incredulously.

"We need at least one person who —"

"You mean, apart from me, you, and Tiffany, meaning all three members of the team, right?" Chronos interrupted.

Kendra let out an exasperated sigh, shaking her head. She didn't even look down. "I mean *useful* magic."

"Right, because my ability to see the future isn't useful at all, which is why you didn't pester me into joining you."

"I mean magical girl magic!" Kendra said. "You're a born mage!"

"And the magical girl powers you and Tiffany both still have don't count because . . .?"

"Because we're not magical girls, we're verges! And I don't have any powers whatsoever!"

Uh huh. Right, Chronos thought, watching Kendra haul herself up to the top step of the ladder and reach high above her head to paint a spot she really shouldn't have attempted. *Either you've got an inhuman sense of balance naturally, which is possible if not probable, or you're using some low-level magic right now without noticing it's there.*

"Oh, I know what you're thinking," Kendra said.

You're remarkably poor at knowing what I'm thinking.

"You're thinking, 'Born mage power is just as good as magical girl power!' But you're wrong."

No, I was wondering if you might be an extremely weak born mage and not know it, Chronos thought. *An unusual sense of balance is exactly the sort of power that's common to weak born mage families. Did you ever volunteer as a police aide? They would have screened for that if you did.*

"A magical girl has no theoretical upper limit on her power," Kendra said pompously. "And she transforms into a second life, meaning she's protected against dying for real. It's the perfect defensive ability, and all magical girls have it. Not to mention the fact that a magical girl can improve when she powers up!"

"Terrific," Chronos muttered. *Why do I care?*

"Tiffany is only a *verge,*" Kendra said, speaking the last word in a tone that was distinctly snobby. "She can't transform or power up. The only way her powers can change is to get weaker as they fade away. You can see why that doesn't count."

"You're a verge, too," Chronos reminded her, finding the scorn with which Kendra had said the word a trifle ridiculous.

"Only technically," Kendra said haughtily, catching the paint can as it teetered and fell. She whipped it around so fast that the paint sloshed back in, and plopped it back on top of the ladder without looking at it. "I have no powers at all."

Uh huh. Right, Chronos thought.

Kendra sighed, a long sigh of frustration. "But Florence said no."

For an instant, Chronos imagined what would have happened if the former magical girl's best friend had agreed to the arrangement. Kendra would have then approached her other teammate, and then every other acquaintance she'd ever known with useful powers, all of whom would have converged upon Chronos's new home in a mass of humanity . . .

Chronos shuddered.

"Good," Chronos repeated, meaning it this time. "I already have too many freeloaders."

Kendra glared at her.

"It wasn't like you even asked me," Chronos began —

"Guess what? Guess what? Guess what?" Tiffany shouted, coming running out of the lair. Her arms were waving wildly, her two braids swinging. "I came up with a *great* team name for us!"

"I fear to ask . . ." Chronos muttered.

Tiffany spread her arms in unbridled joy. "The Daffodils!"

There was a crashing sound as Kendra lost her balance at the top of her ladder. Her paintbrush went flying. Her quick reflexes helped her grab the top of the ladder, and she hung there, swinging, for several seconds.

Not a born mage power, Chronos noted. *Born mages can't turn their magic off, and she lost her balance while distracted.*

"Isn't it perfect?!" Tiffany babbled. "I can use Clyde the Clothing Cupboard to make us all ruffly dresses covered in daffodils —"

"Tiffany . . . we're villains," Chronos said wearily.

Kendra swung to the ground, landing with perfect grace.

"Crocuses?" Tiffany asked hopefully.

"*Villains,*" Kendra said, picking up her fallen paintbrush. The bristles were now coated with strands of dead grass.

"Marigolds?"

"*VILLAINS!*" Chronos and Kendra both shouted.

"Well, I want a better villain name than 'Hey You' this time!" Tiffany sobbed, stomping back into the lair and leaving them behind.

Still not offering to help, I notice, Chronos thought. She watched Kendra climb up the ladder to a new spot, then watched Kendra pick the dead grass out of her paintbrush, wrinkling her nose.

"How about you?" Kendra asked at last, looking up.

Chronos was startled. "How about what?"

"What's your villain name going to be?" Kendra asked.

Chronos blinked. "Chronos."

"Soothsayer," Kendra growled, "that's your regular name."

"Yes," Chronos said, "and?"

"And a regular name is not a villain name!"

Chronos snorted. The former magical girl knew nothing about villains. Chronos's late parents had used their real names; Atlas and Véronique had had no fear of anyone figuring out who they were or where they lived. They would have relished a team of overzealous magical girls trying to attack them in Olympus Estates, but no magical girls had ever been stupid enough to try.

Not yet, anyway, Chronos remembered. *Avenging Angel would have laid waste to Olympus Estates, and the futures with it ending up in ruins aren't entirely gone . . .*

Goosebumps rose on her arms, and she shivered.

Just because she didn't like her family didn't mean she wanted them to all get slaughtered. Even if they did deserve it, seeing as they made a habit of attacking children.

Naturally, Chronos didn't mention any of this. She had no intention of letting Kendra find out she had been raised by a villain family.

"Nobody's ever going to have cause to ask my villain name," Chronos said instead. "I don't want one. Too much bother to remember."

Kendra snorted and rolled her eyes.

"What's yours?" Chronos asked.

Kendra hesitated.

"Dark Cream Angel?" Chronos asked.

"Are you out of your mind?" Kendra gave her an incredulous look. "No! I haven't decided yet."

"You could go by Athena, the goddess of war," Chronos suggested.

"How about no."

"Or maybe Nike, the goddess of victory."

"Isn't that a shoe?"

"Oh, I know!" Chronos snapped her fingers. "Hera! She's always a villain when she shows up!"

"Why are you pulling names from ancient mythology?!"

"Ah . . ." Chronos gulped. "No reason."

"Besides, the only villains who use those names are from that one Olympian family," Kendra muttered.

Chronos flinched. "Is that so?"

Kendra snorted. "It's a good thing your name's not something like those, or I'd've suspected you were one of them."

Chronos's mouth fell open. *Does she not know Chronos is the titan of time?*

Kendra sighed loudly, glaring at the wall as she shoved her paintbrush across a new spot. "It's so frustrating. I want to think of a villain name that sounds cool, but everything I think of is one I've already heard."

"Uh huh," Chronos said carefully. It was still amazing to her that the former magical girl had heard of the Olympian villain family and yet hadn't added up two and two.

"Because I want it to sound *cool,* but I've never studied villain names, you know."

"Right," Chronos said. *I guess I should be glad my dad named me what he did. I hated that he named me after a boy, but if it's proven useful . . .*

"I just want a name that's unique," Kendra griped.

Chronos wrinkled her nose. *You've clearly never been teased because your name was Chronos and your sister's name was Rhea. What kind of sane parents name a pair of siblings after the father and mother of the gods?*

Especially given that Rhea had killed Chronos. Learning that fact had not lessened Chronos's resentment of her name as a child.

Oh, she knew why her parents had done it. Her father's father had started the tradition of naming his children after not just gods but titans, and Atlas had wanted to continue it. When two-year-old Rhea had stopped being able to see anything about her mother's past, and they'd learned shortly afterward that Véronique was pregnant, Atlas had jumped to the correct conclusion that it was due to the second child's power.

Since interference usually only happened when two people were closely related and had similar powers, it had seemed reasonable to assume their second child would be able to see the past like Rhea, or something similar. Therefore, naming the child after the titan of time had made perfect sense. Never mind that the child had ended up being a girl.

"Maybe I'll call myself Nephilim," Kendra mused. "That's a fallen angel in Hebrew mythology, right? Oh, wait, but I think that's plural. And Nephil sounds stupid."

"I thought you didn't want a name from ancient mythology," Chronos said.

"I don't want a name from *Greek* mythology," Kendra said. "Oh! Seraph! That's not a fallen angel, but it's angelic, and it sounds cool. That'll be my name."

Even though she should have kept her mouth shut, Chronos just couldn't let the subject go. "What do you have against Greek mythology?" she demanded.

"Take your pick," Kendra said. "The fact that they forced me to learn it in school, and it was really boring and repetitive? The fact that there's a villain family that worships it?"

Chronos bristled.

"I am *so* glad I learned enough to get a D on that test," Kendra added. She leaned off to the left to paint a new spot. "If I'd failed it, it would've ruined my C average."

"C average?" Chronos sputtered. "How is that possible? Every future I saw of you suggested that you're both smart and an

overachiever!"

"I only care about the things I care about, oracle," Kendra said, as if it were obvious.

Chronos rubbed her forehead.

"Oh, that reminds me," Kendra said, climbing a step higher to paint another cracked spot off to the left. "What was your nightmare about last night?"

Chronos was startled. "How could you —?"

"I'm a light sleeper, and you were mumbling all night."

"But my room's all the way down the hallway!" Chronos exploded.

"Yes," Kendra said. "And I was eavesdropping."

Chronos buried her face in her hands. *Note to self: install soundproofing.*

Chapter 2
The Nightmare

"**W**owww!" Tiffany exclaimed, her eyes wide. "You were in the FBI Special Ops?"

"Yes," Kendra said impatiently. "The Wings of Justice volunteered as FBI aides. Can I get past, please?"

"That makes you famous!" Tiffany cried, waving her arms excitedly, which made her block the hallway even more thoroughly. A dozen broken machines in pieces strewn across the floor were taking care of the rest of the path through the room.

"That makes me *trying to get past you,*" Kendra hinted.

"I've always wanted to be famous," Tiffany said wistfully.

"We weren't famous. Would you please . . ."

"Did you ever get to meet the President?" Tiffany gasped, clasping her hands together.

"I said FBI, not Secret Service!" Kendra snapped. "The magical girl aides for the Secret Service are *way* more elite! Now would you please *move?*"

Looking reluctant, Tiffany moved aside. But after Kendra squeezed past her to get to the stairs, the verge trailed after her, peppering her with questions.

"Did you ever get to beat a bad guy? Do the magical girls use guns, or just agents? Is it like you see in the cartoons on TV?"

Kendra felt her cheek twitch. It was enough to make her contemplate digging the watch out of her pocket so that she could teleport away.

"I saw a really fun cartoon the other day," Tiffany said. She burst out into the theme song: *"Magical Girl Rent-a-cop! Saves the mall while others shop —"*

"Okay, stop!" Kendra burst out. "First of all, it was not fixing the TVs when you made them incapable of showing anything but cartoons. Second, that show is awful. Third, have you seen the oracle anywhere? I think she's hiding from me."

"She told me not to say where she was hiding," Tiffany said.

Kendra whirled around and gave the girl a sharp glare.

"Do you want to help me rebuild Brian?" Tiffany asked hopefully. "I went to lots of effort to make him, and then Chronos made me break him and took half the pieces away."

"No, I'm not going to help you rebuild the brainwasher," Kendra growled. "Where's the oracle hiding?"

"I dunno . . ." Tiffany sang, tapping a finger against her lips. "Somewhere . . ."

Kendra closed her eyes. She was not going to put dangerous weapons back into the hands of this brat, but perhaps she could bargain with something else.

"I'll tell you about my time in the FBI," she said, opening her eyes, "if you'll tell me where the oracle's hiding."

Tiffany's eyes brightened. "Were you famous? Did you get your picture on TV?"

"Well, it certainly wouldn't have shown up on your cartoons-only TVs," Kendra muttered.

"What's a handler?" Tiffany added.

Kendra sighed explosively. She'd made the mistake of yelling, *"Even our FBI handler gave us more information than you've been giving me, soothsayer!"* while looking for Chronos, which was how she'd gotten into this mess.

"Is it like a door handle?" Tiffany asked. "Could I fix it?"

Kendra had not parted with their FBI handler on the best of terms. "Yes," she said. "I'd love to see you try to fix it."

Tiffany grinned and summoned her wand.

"We were only helping the FBI in our first year," Kendra explained. "We quit after we killed the drug lord."

Or more specifically, after Kendra had killed the drug lord instead of taking him prisoner, like they'd agreed to do. And after Florence had taken it upon herself to scream at their handler for having secretly encouraged Kendra to do that because there were no investigations over kills by magical girls.

"Can I fix the handler?" Tiffany asked.

"It's not here," Kendra said. *I'm pretty sure he'd never work with us again, even if I begged him.* Which she wouldn't do, because she'd said some pretty choice words herself after he had yelled right back at Florence about her being too naive.

Overall, that had been a really bad day. And even though she'd quit being a magical girl, it still rankled that she'd never gotten a second chance to go back there because Florence had been stubborn about it.

Florence. Kendra's stomach clenched. She still couldn't believe her best friend had turned her down.

Was there something else she could have said to persuade her? Kendra had had it all worked out. Maybe if Florence had just listened to the details and known that she'd have a secret identity and be able to live at home and just be on call whenever needed . . .

No, Kendra thought. She felt sick. *She thought I was exactly the same as Lute Deathwave. That look of betrayal on her face — it was exactly the same. There was nothing I could have said to persuade her.*

Perhaps she should have anticipated that, but she hadn't. To Kendra, the choice to become a villain had been clear and necessary, the only logical conclusion to reach. She'd naturally assumed that once Florence heard the reasons, she would see what had to be done.

Apparently not.

"We started out as aides for the local police," Kendra said, remembering the good times with wistfulness. "We wound up going back to that afterwards. Well, sometimes. That wasn't all we did."

"Wow!" Tiffany cried. "My team never even registered!"

Kendra blinked and stared at her. "They didn't?"

"Nuh uh." Tiffany shook her head.

Kendra rubbed her forehead. "That's illegal if you're going to fight humans, you know. Please tell me they weren't fighters."

"They beat up a bully at school once," Tiffany said eagerly. "Does that count?"

"Yes."

Tiffany's eyes brightened. "You mean I could get my team in trouble?!"

Kendra snorted. "Not as long as everyone thinks you're dead."

Tiffany pouted deeply. "Awwwwww . . ."

Kendra stared at the ten-year-old girl with exasperation. *That* was the only reason she would be tempted to go back home? "Haven't you ever heard of 'team loyalty'?"

"I'm not being loyal to them!" Tiffany burst out indignantly. "Every chance they got, they made fun of me!"

"Why would they do that?" Kendra asked.

"I dunnooooooooo!" Tiffany wailed. "I became a magical girl because they were, but then they still didn't like me!"

In other words, Kendra thought, *you weren't invited onto the team, and yet, you insisted on horning your way in anyway?*

"Well, you probably deserved it," Kendra said.

"Nuh uh!" Tiffany wailed, her eyes filling with tears. "I was the victim! They were ten, and I was only four, and no one ever wanted to include me!"

"No doubt because you were a pest."

"I wasn't a pest! I was *adorable!*" Tiffany shouted.

The ten-year-old proceeded to begin a rant about how everything was unfair and Chronos had made her take some of her dangerous machine-friends apart and Chronos had gone hiding in the dungeons and she hadn't even invited Tiffany to play there with her —

The dungeons, Kendra thought. *Great!*

She shoved her hand in her pocket, pulled out the watch, and teleported out of the overstuffed hallway outside of Tiffany's room, landing in the middle of the dungeons.

The Nightmare

She looked around at the now bare and empty room. Apart from posters and a bit of clutter their former prisoner hadn't bothered to clear out, it now looked uninhabited. The cavernous space of cages looked enormous, the emptiness beyond the bars gaping to be filled.

Kendra shivered.

She walked around, checking every corner of the room, but it was empty. If Chronos had been hiding here, she was in a different room. Kendra teleported back upstairs, looking around for her next clue, and finally caught a glimpse of movement at the corner of her eye in the plotting room.

Aha! Kendra thought.

"So . . ." she said, walking right in and flopping into a chair across the table from Chronos, who was reading a book. "When are you going to tell me who we're fighting?"

Chronos looked up, her expression irritable. "For one thing, there is no 'we.' I don't fight anybody."

"Right, right," Kendra said, waving her hand. "So tell me who *I'm* fighting."

"I never said you were going to be fighting," Chronos said, drumming her fingers on the table. "Just because I had a bad dream doesn't mean there's anything for you do to about it."

Kendra brushed that objection aside. "Please. You saw a nightmare future, and you *don't* want me to fix it? Get real."

"Most of the futures I see have nothing to do with your people!" Chronos snapped. "Good or bad! This might amaze you to hear, but magical girls aren't at the center of everything!"

"Duh," Kendra said. "But you said '*Sonnenkinder*' last night. I speak German. That means 'magical girl.'"

Chronos rubbed her forehead.

Bingo, Kendra thought, leaning forward with eagerness.

"You speak German?" Chronos asked.

Kendra sat back in annoyance, putting her feet on the table and crossing her legs. That wasn't the point here. "Sure. We lived a year in Hamburg while Mom was writing Sunny's biography."

"And that was enough to be fluent?" Chronos asked.

"I was in first grade," Kendra shrugged. "I cared about schoolwork back then. Duh."

For some reason, Chronos looked exasperated.

"Now, stop dodging the question," Kendra said. "What was your nightmare about?"

Chronos shook her head slowly, displaying both sides of her messily unbrushed hair. "You seem to think violence is a solution. There are some things it can't fix."

"Not things that you have nightmares about," Kendra said.

"Oh, do you think?" Chronos asked acidly. "It's good to know that when I foresee natural disasters, marital infidelities, outbreaks of diseases, or food shortages in poor countries, all I'll ever need to do is call upon you to go slice-and-dice somebody."

Kendra was silent for a moment.

Chronos picked up her book.

"Which one of those was it?" Kendra asked.

Chronos opened her book with determination.

"I mean, you mentioned something about a magical girl," Kendra said. "Does one *cause* a natural disaster, disease outbreak, food shortage, or marital infidelity?"

Chronos put the book in front of her face and didn't answer.

"Right," Kendra said, getting up. "I guess I'll just have to go attack a magical girl who has strong earth-based powers in case she's about to cause an earthquake. Since you said *Sonnenkinder,* that means she's probably German. Schönwasser lives in Berlin, doesn't she?"

"Oh, for crying out loud!" Chronos exploded. "It's nothing like that!"

"Yes?" Kendra said.

Chronos shut her book and glowered.

Kendra waited, grinning.

"It's . . . it's just a child. A bully," Chronos muttered. She held out her left hand to display a girl with black, curly hair. The girl wore a blouse with a rounded collar in the front that fell in a long, rounded piece in the back. "I don't like bullies, that's all. She's no threat. Just arrogant. The world doesn't need saving —"

"Huh. That's a Rouen Académie des Saintes uniform," Kendra interrupted. "The school for magical girls in France."

Chronos blinked. "Well —"

Kendra pushed back her chair, stood up, and got to her feet. "See ya!"

"*Kendra!*" Chronos shouted. "She's *seven years old!*"

Not caring, Kendra was already teleporting away.

Chapter 3
The Mission

Given that she didn't speak French, Kendra's first action was to teleport back to her home library to steal a French-English dictionary. She'd need to construct a few sentences to be able to communicate. She couldn't assume that a seven-year-old would speak English.

Running her finger along the spines in the reference section, ducking down and hoping nobody walked past and saw her face, Kendra grabbed the book and was about to teleport out.

"Are you sure it'll work?" a voice giggled.

Kendra froze. What was Felicity doing here? As far as she knew, her ditzy third teammate had never set foot in a library.

"Trust me," another girl's voice said confidently. "All you need is a makeover, and this book on makeup tips is just the thing."

Kendra snorted, but otherwise stayed frozen and tense.

"Thank you so much for helping me!" Felicity's voice effused as two pairs of feet walked past the bookcase Kendra was hiding behind.

Kendra held her breath, but neither set of footsteps slowed.

"Of course," the other girl said. "What are best friends for?"

Best friends? Kendra's brow wrinkled. *Since when? Who is that girl?*

She crawled to the edge of the bookcase and peered around the corner. She caught sight of a pair of purple sneakers disappearing into another room.

Oh, Kendra realized. *Right.* It was Tess, one of Felicity's friends from elementary school. Kendra knew the two of them had been hanging out together a lot since Tess had moved back into town over summer vacation. She hadn't known that they called each other best friends, though.

What else has changed? Kendra thought. Indignation swelled in her chest. *I've only been gone a week!*

What if this was why Florence hadn't wanted to join her? What if she'd waited too long, and Florence had already found a new best friend?

No, no, no, Kendra told herself firmly. *Florence is ridiculously cautious, especially after Lute Deathwave. She wouldn't make a new friend that easily, especially not one that could replace me.*

But what if?

What if nobody missed her at all?

Did I do the wrong thing? Kendra wondered, squeezing the dictionary. *If Florence thinks so . . .*

But no. Florence was wrong. It was just like their FBI handler had said: she was too naive, and had too little understanding of the sacrifices that had to be made for the greater good. Sometimes you had to kill a bad guy to make sure his lawyers wouldn't keep him out of prison again. Sometimes you had to be a villain to save the world from overpowered magical girls.

She heard another pair of footsteps coming towards her, and Kendra quickly teleported out. If it had been her parents acting normal, as if nothing had changed, she didn't think she could have borne it.

Kendra sat on the roof of the Rouen Académie des Saintes building, hidden in a nook between one of the towers and one of the small chimney tubes that had probably once been functional, but was now only decorative.

She'd been here for hours, trying to puzzle out French sentence structure and grammar, which made no sense to her. And what was with all of those extra letters? Were they supposed to be silent or what? Not to mention the pronunciation. She was certain she'd butcher that.

Okay, Kendra thought, reviewing the three sentences she'd planned out. *I think I can say those. That should make it clear. Now, when the kids arrive . . .*

She held onto the skinny chimney and leaned forward to peer around the side of the tower. There were children arriving outside the school now, elementary-aged girls wearing the same ruffled uniform.

Bingo, Kendra thought. *Now which one is the one I need?*

She wished this had been the Berlin Schüle für Sonnenkinder. She would have known her way around there. She'd considered asking her parents to move to Berlin during her high school years so that she could attend it, which was why she had kept her German in practice. Those plans had dissipated after Florence had decided to become a magical girl and they'd formed a team together, but still.

Why had Chronos said *"Sonnenkinder"* if the bully was in France, anyway? The French word for "magical girl" was the incredibly pretentious *"sainte,"* which also meant "saint." The German language was far more practical. *"Sonnenkinder"* meant "sun children," a reference to the first magical girl, Sunny.

Of course, *"sainte"* at least had the feminine "the," while *"Sonnenkind"* used the neuter one, which was almost as annoying as the fact that *"Mädchen"* (girl) was a neuter word . . .

Focus, Kendra told herself sternly.

She didn't see any girls down below who had shoulder length, dark, curly hair, but it suddenly occurred to her that Chronos had been showing her the future, not the present — the girl could have a completely different hairstyle right now.

It probably would've helped if she had gotten the girl's name, but going back for more information hadn't been an option, not after making such a cool exit. Besides, Chronos wouldn't have told her.

Great, Kendra thought, shielding her eyes. The sun was shining right in her field of vision. *They all look alike from here. Which one is the bully? And does she speak a word of English?*

She refused to go home as a failure. This was her first mission. She had to make it spectacular.

Maybe Chronos said "Sonnenkinder" because she was dreaming about the rivalry between the two schools! Kendra realized.

If that was true, the dream about this particular magical girl had probably been before or after that point, which meant Kendra had been lucky to hear the word at all.

How many other dreams has the oracle had that she's been hiding from me? Kendra thought irritably. *How am I supposed to know when there's something important?*

She envied Chronos's power. If she'd had the ability to see the future, she would have used it long ago to fix all of the world's problems. Imagine having access to that kind of information all day every day!

Of course, if she'd had Chronos's power, that would have made her a born mage. Kendra shuddered at the idea. She was very glad she wasn't one of those things. She had known she wasn't, of course, but she had still been relieved when the FBI had tested her at the beginning and found her clean.

Was Sunny a born mage? Kendra wondered.

She hoped not. Everyone knew that born mages were evil. But then again, it was indisputable that most of the early magical girls had been born mages, probably because small children who already knew how to use magic were the ones who had first grasped the idea of using a new magic system.

So clearly not all born mages were evil. Just most of them. She was fairly certain Chronos wasn't, for instance.

Still, the thought of Sunny having been a born mage made Kendra uncomfortable. It was one of the leading theories about the mysterious first magical girl, about whom very little was known, but it was definitely not the theory Kendra preferred.

Another leading theory was that Sunny had come from another world. Kendra didn't mind that one, though it wasn't her favorite.

Her *favorite* theory was the idea that the world itself had conceived magical girls in response to the corruptions of born mages, a way to make magic something open and virtuous rather than evil and secret. The magic system had been created to end the Great War, after all, the War to End All Wars, in 1915.

Most of the other theories revolved around particular religions, and Kendra dismissed most of those. Muslims and Jews both believed Sunny had been a messenger from God. Buddhists tended to consider her a *bodhisattva*. Some Catholics had argued that she should be made a saint, despite having been Lutheran. Pagans believed that she had been a god herself.

Kendra had once asked Florence what she thought Sunny had been. Florence's response had been a succinct: *"How the heck should I know? Does it really matter, anyway?"*

It matters, Kendra thought. *Of course it matters. Especially now that I know the magic system isn't as incorruptible as I used to believe.*

A little girl with shoulder-length, curly dark hair walked onto the school grounds, waving goodbye to a dark, curly-haired mother.

Ahhh, Kendra thought, standing up and dropping the dictionary. *Now to wait for the perfect opening.*

Ellen trudged onto the playground where half the other girls were currently playing, clutching her huge heart-shaped wand for emotional support.

She'd begged her parents to let her go to a school for magies back home, but there hadn't been one in Perth, and her parents hadn't been willing to let her go to boarding school in Brisbane. But then her dad had gotten news that he was going to be sent to Rouen for work. Rouen, where the very first school for magical girls had started!

Ellen's begging had immediately switched into overdrive.

"Please, Mum! Please, Dad! I have to go to Rouen Académie des Saintes! Please, Mum! Please, Dad! Pleeeeeeeeeeeeease!"

The Mission

Despite the fact that her French had been horrible, the school had taken her in, on the condition that she attend summer school and take remedial classes until she was up to the same level as the other girls her age. Ellen had been thrilled.

But no one wanted to be friends with her.

Ellen held on to the huge plastic wand tightly. That was why she'd bought this at a toy store with her birthday money. That was why she was going to pretend she'd powered up and this was her new focus item, so all the other girls would "ooh" and "ahh," and it wouldn't matter that she spoke French so horribly.

Glancing across the playground in front of the school, Ellen caught sight of Juliette saying goodbye to her mother. Her fingers tightened around the wand, and her hands shook.

Don't notice me . . . she thought. *Everybody else, please see my wand be impressed, but Juliette, don't notice me . . .*

Too late. The most popular girl in the non-remedial class for her age group had turned around and seen her. Ellen tried to hide the enormous wand behind her back, but that only made Juliette grin and hurry over.

"What's that?" the popular girl mocked. *"Did you buy that at a toy store?"*

What's she saying? Ellen thought frantically. Juliette always talked too fast for her to understand. *Did she say the word "toy"?*

Just in case, Ellen frantically shook her head. *"I power up the new . . . thing,"* she said in broken French. *"Thing of magic doing."*

Juliette burst out laughing. *"You don't expect me to believe that's your new focus item, do you? I've seen that in a toy store!"*

Ellen blinked back tears. Why was Juliette always so mean? Why couldn't she understand a word Juliette was saying?

"You're a wicked liar, and liars shouldn't be saintes," Juliette said, snatching the huge plastic wand away from her.

"Give me!" Ellen cried, diving for it.

"Ask grammatically first!" Juliette taunted, holding it high above her head. She was taller, so she could do that.

Ellen didn't understand her. *"Give me!"*

"Ask grammatically," Juliette growled.

Ellen leapt up and smacked the wand, which tumbled out of Juliette's grip. She lunged for it, but Juliette stomped her foot on top of it.

"Give me!" Ellen wailed, trying to yank it free.

"You're stupid!" Juliette shouted. *"And you're ugly! Someone should make you talk properly!"*

Ellen yanked her enormous plastic wand free and tumbled backwards. She clutched the wand to her chest, shouting one of the few things she knew how to say. *"Juliette's MEAN!"*

Then, because that wasn't enough, she started shouting it in English, too.

"Mean, mean, mean, mean, MEAN!"

High above their heads, Kendra was startled.

English? An Australian accent . . .? Excitement dawned. *Hey, great! That girl can translate for me!*

There was an adult Kendra hadn't noticed before moving to separate the two girls, probably a teacher, so Kendra would have to move quickly.

Now, if only she hadn't lost track of the girl with dark, curly hair a minute ago. Her target had been right . . .

Oh. Kendra felt a little idiotic. *Annnd the bully's with her. That's convenient.*

There was an adult Kendra hadn't noticed before moving to separate the two girls, probably a teacher, so she'd have to move quickly. This was likely the best opportunity she would get.

Kendra dove off the building, flipped in midair, and landed in a crouch. That was something she had gotten very good at during her days as a magical girl. She pulled back her arm with the spiky halo . . .

"VILLAIN!" a dozen voices shouted, and a dozen weapons shoved right into her face.

Oh, great, Kendra thought.

She had to admire the creativity of the weapons surrounding her. One looked like a lance with swirling clouds twisting around it. One looked like a cross between a tiara and a frisbee. One was a sword with pearls and ruffles on the handle. One was a shotgun with a teddy bear hanging from it.

She didn't admire all of them. The huge plastic wand looked like it had come straight out of a toy store, and the lacy glove and diamond-encrusted scarf were lame.

Kendra leapt straight above their heads, flipped in midair, and landed several feet away. "I'm not a typical villain!" she called. "I only fight *corrupt* magical girls!"

The circle of magical girls all had blank stares.

"You," Kendra said, jabbing her thumb in the direction of the Australian girl. "Translate."

"Me?!" the girl yelped.

"YOU!" Kendra shouted.

"Um . . ." the girl said, her eyes wide. She looked around as if still hoping Kendra was talking to someone else. "Ummm . . . *Not bad girl. Fight bad saintes?*" she said hesitantly.

The blank looks shifted to an assortment of angry, confused, and offended. Several girls shouted comments in French.

Satisfied that her message had gotten through,

Not waiting for the response, Kendra bolted over, grabbed the bully by the back of her collar, and held the spiked halo threateningly at the girl's throat. "Now, let's talk about bullying your classmates."

"*She's threatening to kill Juliette!*" the girl holding the frisbee-tiara screamed.

Chomp. Kendra screamed herself and flung the bully away from her, too startled at being bitten to think clearly.

The little girl transformed in midair into a magical girl with antennae and butterfly wings. A stream of angry butterflies shot towards her.

"*Die, villain!*"

Kendra dodged to the left, but the diamond-encrusted scarf swung forward like a hissing snake. She rolled to the right, but lightning flashed by her. She leapt in the air, but flowers bloomed from nowhere and exploded into large fireworks.

This is not working!

A wall of autumn leaves burst past her.

Lightning smashed against the ground exactly where she had been a second earlier.

A wave of pink hearts surrounded her.

Bullets whammed past, wrapped in some sort of — poison mist?

Kendra leapt in the air, flipped forward, and landed in front of her translator.

"Explain it to them!" she shouted, knocking the plastic wand the girl aimed at her aside. "I just have to stop the bully! If I kill her magical girl form, she'll never bother you again —"

The little girl's eyes glowed, and she reached into her pocket and pulled out a silver bracelet.

Light flashed.

Kendra gasped, realizing she was blinded. In her moment of incapacitation, the diamond-encrusted scarf lashed around her arm, lifting her in the air. A crackling of thunder began above her —

"Teleport!" Kendra screamed.

She landed on her rear end on the floor of their lair.

"I take it trying to fight an entire school of magical girls was a stupid idea?" Chronos asked calmly, walking past with a sandwich in her hand.

"Shut up!" Kendra snapped, checking herself over for injuries. There were, unfortunately, a lot of them. Minor cuts, awful bruises, and worst of all, a slice right through her left boot. She couldn't simply detransform and retranform and heal her costume that way.

Tiffany's power could probably fix it, Kendra thought. *But ugh, if I ask her for a favor, that'll be like admitting that she's really part of our team . . .*

"May I suggest, next time, that you not try to trick your way into a mission I don't intend to send you on?" Chronos asked, looking distinctly smug.

Kendra glowered at the born mage. "It wasn't the mission that was the problem! It was the language barrier that was the problem!"

"Then, helpful hint," Chronos said dryly: "don't pick fights with people who don't speak your language."

"Or at least hire translators who know what they're doing!" Kendra said furiously. "I don't think that girl was even trying!"

"Or that," Chronos said cheerfully.

"It's too bad we don't have someone on our team who speaks French," Kendra muttered as the soothsayer ambled away.

Chronos hid a grin as she slipped into the plotting room to return to the crochet project she had been working on. She spoke fluent French, given that her mother had been French, but she wasn't going to volunteer that to Kendra.

She checked the futures at the Rouen Académie des Saintes. It looked like Ellen was going to be the center of attention for several weeks, having dealt the decisive blow to the unknown villain, and eventually she and Juliette were going to end up friends because Juliette thought Ellen had saved her life.

Not bad, all things considered. And Kendra being humiliated was just a bonus.

Chapter 4
The Dream

Two friends were talking.

"You didn't know that Joan of Arc is the patron saint of magical girls?" the girl with blonde hair was saying in a snobby, know-it-all voice.

"No," the black girl said defensively. "Should I have?"

"You're the one who's Christian," the white girl smirked. "You ought to know stuff about your own religion."

"I'm not Catholic!" the dark-skinned girl snapped. "Why would I know that, or care?"

The scene changed. Both girls looked a year or so older.

"Don't you love it?" the black girl was squealing, holding up a handful of tiny braids.

"What was wrong with dreadlocks?" the white girl complained. "I told you you should get those!"

"And I decided I'd prefer braids," the black girl snapped.

"Should *I* do my hair in dreadlocks?" an anxious-looking girl asked from beside them, twirling a pair of brown pigtails on either side of her shoulders.

"NO!" both of her friends said immediately.

The scene changed. All three friends looked older, and the brown-haired girl now wore her hair in a shorter ponytail.

"And he's so cute, and his name is Daniel!" the brown-haired girl was squealing, barely stopping to take a breath. "I think I'm in love! It's true love!"

The black girl scowled, took a french fry off her cafeteria tray, and took a vicious bite.

"Maybe talking about love in front of Florence is not the best idea right now . . ." the blonde girl said nervously, glancing over at her scowling friend.

"But it's true love!" the brown-haired girl squealed.

The black girl stood abruptly and walked away from the table.

The scene changed. Now all three girls looked a year older, and the blonde one looked close to tears.

"I've decided . . . to become . . . a villain instead."

The halo the blonde girl was holding grew spikes. Thick iron spikes jabbed out of the gold ring.

"WHAT?!" her two friends shouted.

"If magical girls can betray the world, then someone has to stop them!" the blonde girl shouted. "So as of right now, I'm officially defecting!"

"Are you insane?" the black girl yelped.

"*Teleport!*" the blonde girl screamed, raising the spiked halo and a watch that looked very familiar over her head.

The scene changed. Not looking any older at all, the blonde girl was now wearing a very familiar villain costume.

"Explain it to them!" she was shouting. "I just have to stop the bully! If I kill her magical girl form, she'll never bother you again —"

A little girl reached into her pocket and pulled out a tiny silver bracelet. A blinding light flashed, and it was instantly obvious the blonde girl had been blinded.

"Teleport!" the blonde girl shouted again. Then the scene slid away as if careening into something impossible to see.

Rhea awoke.

Rhea blinked, a little fuzzy-headed due to having just been asleep. *Huh . . . I remember that costume . . . who did I make it for?*

She sat up, yawned, and spread her hands before her. Her memory was quite good, but not when she'd just been asleep.

"*Nothing* about when I made it?" she muttered out loud.

That made no sense. Rhea's power always worked. Except for — *Oh! Of course! I made it when Chronos was there!*

Rhea giggled. She should have remembered immediately. She'd had such fun with those buckles. If she hadn't been asleep, she would have recognized it immediately.

A slow smile spread across Rhea's face.

Rhea's dreams were never dreams. They were her born mage gift acting out of control. Rhea could see the past, which wasn't the best part.

The best part was that it never *stopped.*

Rhea beamed as she settled into a comfortable position with her hands folded on her lap. The only problem with her power was that she couldn't always find what she wanted if she didn't know enough specifics to look for. The chaotic, random nature of her dreams often brought things to her attention that she would never have known to look for before.

For the past two months, she had been searching for her sister's defector, but she'd had nothing to go on except the costume she'd made, which hadn't been enough. If her sister had been anyone else, she could have searched through Chronos's past to find a common scene between them, but her sister was annoyingly immune to her power.

I'm glad the defector isn't spending all *her time with Chronos,* Rhea thought with satisfaction. *Now let's see how much of her past will be laid bare to me.*

Rhea started from the beginning, since she was in no hurry and context was everything. She scanned through the girl's early years at high speed, seeing nothing interesting, and stopped only to watch one of the newly-transformed magical girl's first battles against the most pathetic-looking villains Rhea had ever seen.

Rhea's eyebrows rose. *The Terrifying Flea-Boys? Really?*

She had never seen those villains before, but if she had, she would have advised them to name themselves after something that didn't sound like a minor pest just waiting to be swatted. And then there was the atrocity of their costumes, which were prison jumpsuits with enormous flea wings stitched on, as if they were some sort of winged magical girl wannabes.

On a whim, seeing Kendra with her parents, Rhea flicked back to see what her parents' pasts were. Her mother had apparently been a dull, insipid magical girl singer — nothing interesting there. Her father had been a Deathwave minion, which had *fantastic* blackmail possibilities, but then she discovered that he'd already confessed that to the police and gotten his boss thrown in prison decades ago. Quite a disappointment.

Returning to Kendra, Rhea skimmed through three years of the magical girl's aggravatingly superior attitude, then landed headlong into a scene she couldn't reach.

Wha —?

Rhea stared at her hands in bafflement.

This has to be the point where she and my sister met. But why? I can't see any reason why Chronos would have chosen this girl. No reason that girl would become a defector, either.

Rhea shook her head. There was no point in trying to extrapolate before she'd watched everything she could. Perhaps this had just been a chance meeting, and Chronos had returned with a good reason later.

But no. When Kendra became visible again, the girl was noticeably shaken, sobbing as she walked home.

What in the world?! Rhea's mouth fell open. *How did my sister break that irritating arrogance?*

She skimmed backwards again, desperate for some clue, but there was nothing. She skimmed forward, and at last found one single hint: "The world *does* need me to save it. I see . . ."

Rhea stared at her hands. That made even less sense than before. What was going on here?

There had been no empty spaces before this, which meant that Chronos had started whatever had happened.

Chronos had started it.

Chronos had come out of hiding in order to do it.

And wait a minute — was that Chronos's watch? How had the defector gotten that?!

Rhea closed her eyes and took a deep breath. Okay, it was a mystery, and one she couldn't simply clear up by asking her sister, because Chronos tended to get surly and refuse to answer questions about anything. Perhaps it would be best to enjoy what she *could* do right now, which was to see what the defector was currently doing.

She snorted with laughter as she saw a political rally in which Kendra swooped down and broke the focus items of both magical girls posing and performing on behalf of their party's candidates.

She chuckled at the undercover magical girl police aide Kendra blew the cover of.

She howled at the two magical girl friends who started fighting one another as soon as Kendra left.

Rhea skipped around randomly, hopping from one scene to another, not bothering to watch them all the way through.

"I wonder what else her defector's been up to?" Rhea giggled. "Hee hee! I love spying!"

For extra fun, she skipped as far to the future as possible, finding a scene from early yesterday, when Kendra had killed —

— the magical girl form of Crackling Bluejay?!

Rhea's hands went numb. She'd spent months carefully corrupting that magical girl, leading her to believe that magic and her family's poor financial situation (which Rhea had triggered) gave her the right to steal anything she pleased. All that effort, the lovely inevitable backlash against magical girls that would have happened when Rhea made sure the police "accidentally" caught her in the act . . . gone.

No sense of the big picture, Rhea thought angrily. *Can't she see that that particular magical girl was worth more to villains alive than dead? She was fencing half of her profits to the Deathwaves, for crying out loud!*

Rhea flipped back to a scene that had made her laugh, wanting something to cool her rage.

But it wasn't funny the second time. Not when she watched it all the way through.

The embarrassment of a villain swooping down and breaking both Red Elephant and Blue Donkey's focus items had caused the police to tighten up security tremendously. At the next rally, that had made the difference in their stopping an unanticipated assassination attempt.

The magical girls who had started fighting after Kendra left had also been fighting before Kendra came. And then Kendra had come back, beaten them both, and forced them to apologize to one another.

The undercover magical girl whose cover Kendra had blown had been secretly taking bribes. Once her cover was blown and she was pulled off the investigation, she stopped being able to sabotage it. And then, as if to be completely unambiguous about the fact that she had done that on purpose, Kendra had called the police with an anonymous tip about the bribe-accepting.

Worst of all was when Rhea found the defector's first mission, which turned out to have been the final scene in her dream:

"I'm not a typical villain! I only fight *corrupt* magical girls!"

Rhea went still. *No . . .*

She went back to check the other scenes thoroughly. And sure enough, the hints were all there.

"If you'd used your powers for *good,* then I wouldn't be breaking this."

New scene.

"You killed my magical girl form! Without it, I'm *nothing!*"

"You're not convincing me you're stable enough to handle magic."

New scene.

"And now you will apologize for fighting one another!"

"*Sorrrrry . . .*"

New scene.

"Hello, Chicago police? I thought you'd like to know Wisteria has been taking bribes."

No, Rhea thought, breathing heavily. *No.*

She raced back to the original blank space, looking for any hint that she'd missed. And at last, she found one. One lone scene in two weeks of blankness, shining in the emptiness like a jewel of clarity.

"I didn't want to quit." Kendra traced her finger in a circle around the knee of her jeans, speaking to the black girl who had been her best friend in so much of her past before Chronos. "I really didn't want to defect. But . . . I found out . . . it's possible for magical girls to turn corrupt. One with sufficient charisma and arrogance could even lead the world to destruction. That would have been my future. A born mage showed me. So I . . ."

"You listened to a *born mage?*" her friend exploded. "After all the things you said to me about Lute Deathwave? Are you crazy? *Obviously* he was lying!"

"No, she wasn't!" Kendra snapped. Her feet stomped back on the floor, and she planted an accusing finger forward. "I became a villain for the same reason we both became magical girls: to protect world peace!"

Rhea's hands jerked, and she stopped the vision.

"She . . . became . . . a villain . . . to . . ."

It was unreasonable. It was unthinkable. It was unbelievable.

It was so very, very Chronos.

". . . to cull out the corrupt?!" Rhea exploded. "That'll only make the others *more* powerful!"

She couldn't believe her sister would do this. She knew it went against everything the Olympians stood for. Enemies were supposed to be destroyed or eroded, not *improved.*

"Wait . . . does Chronos know about this?" Rhea muttered.

It was possible she didn't. Kendra could simply have gone rogue. Chronos might be clueless enough that, despite her power, she had somehow failed to figure out what the defector was doing.

It was hard to believe that anyone could be that clueless, but if anyone could, it would be Chronos.

Rhea opened her hands, skimmed back to the start of the scene, and watched and listened carefully until she reached the same place she'd stopped at before.

The Dream

"I found out . . . it's possible for magical girls to turn corrupt. One with sufficient charisma and arrogance could even lead the world to destruction. That would have been my future. A born mage showed me. So I . . ."

Rhea clenched her fists until the knuckles turned white.

"She knew," she whispered in a deadly voice. "She started this when she *knew*."

Chronos was a traitor.

Zazz gulped her drink and handed it back to the bartender. "Another one, please!" she said brightly, swinging her arrowhead tail back and forth. The people of her world weren't capable of getting drunk, but she enjoyed the flavor of alcohol. The way it burned on the way down made her giggle.

Sipping her next drink, she headed over to a table where she leaned back in a chair to watch the party with a grin on her face. Minion bars were the best. Nobody cared that she had a tail here — in fact, there were plenty of guys who thought it was sexy.

"So then I built this death ray . . ." a bearded man in a cloak was saying.

"Ha ha!" the woman across from him giggled flirtatiously.

Zazz downed her drink and got another. Working as Rhea's shopgirl could be a drag. She had to pretend to be sweet and helpful, even when she wanted to smack stupid customers upside the head, and her tail was always stiff after a day of keeping it hidden under her skirt. She didn't even get to use her real name. She had to go by "Minerva," some goddess of wisdom from this world or something, because her real name was so common in her home world that it would have been a dead giveaway where she was from, and Rhea was a quiet villain, not an open one. Blargh.

But here, in a minion bar, she could relax. Here, surrounded by Deathwaves and otherworlders and born mages independents, she could be herself and do as she pleased.

She finished her drink. "Another!" she yelled.

"*Zazz! Phone!*" someone called out over the crowd, waving a large bricklike object at her.

"Hmm?" Zazz turned around.

"Phone," the man repeated, dropping the bricklike thing in her hand.

Zazz stared at the thing with a sinking feeling. There was only one person who was guaranteed to know exactly where she was and how to reach her at all times.

Her boss was calling.

"*Rhea!* It's my day *off!*" she protested, not waiting for the person on the other end to speak up.

"Take tomorrow instead," her boss said. "I need you today."

"But I don't want to deal with customers!" Zazz whined.

"No customers today," Rhea said in a clipped voice. "I'm closing the shop."

Zazz was shocked into silence. Her boss never closed the shop, not even on Christmas, a holiday in this world that was apparently a big deal, but not to Rhea. She'd missed quite a lot of parties because her boss wouldn't give her time off for them.

Zazz frowned. "Isn't that the one who you say never answers the door?"

"That's the one."

"The one who moved out of the apartment you knew about?"

"That's the one."

"I thought you didn't know where to find her now."

"I didn't bother to try," her boss said coldly. "It took me less than an hour once I went looking. A realtor I know recently sold a lair to someone using my sister's name. I checked. I can't see inside it. That means it's certain Chronos is there."

"And we're going to visit?" Zazz asked.

"Yes." Rhea's voice was cold.

There was something strange about this. What was the rush? Why was her boss closing her shop? Why did Rhea sound so angry?

"Boss," Zazz said cautiously, "is something wrong?"

There was a long pause.

"Yes," Rhea said. "I think my sister is a traitor."

Zazz's eyes widened. She'd never seen her boss deal with a traitor, probably because every villain or minion knew it was impossible to double-cross her, but she had no doubt what Rhea would do.

"So we're going there to . . .?" she asked slowly.

"So we're going there," Rhea said in a clipped voice, not answering her minion's unspoken question. "Today."

www.ingramcontent.com/pod-product-compliance
Lightning Source LLC
Chambersburg PA
CBHW022044050726
47591CB00003B/940